Geraldine's
Rainy Day

Nina Reginelli
Illustrated by Ben Guse

For Esther and Samuel

ISBN: 978-1-77069-281-7

Word Alive Press
131 Cordite Road, Winnipeg, MB R3W 1S1
www.wordalivepress.ca

WORD ALIVE PRESS
Just Write!

Library and Archives Canada Cataloguing in Publication

Reginelli, Nina, 1965-

Geraldine's rainy day / Nina Reginelli.

ISBN 978-1-77069-281-7

I. Title.

PS8635.E393G47 2011   jC813'.6   C2011-902435-7

This book belongs to

_____

It was a rainy summer day. Geraldine, the giraffe, was at home playing with her baby brother, Geronimo. They enjoyed chasing each other around like a cat after a mouse. They would get so excited that they would shout from the top of their lungs.

Mommy stepped in and said, "Time for your nap, Geronimo."

Geraldine caught her breath and said sadly,

"Already!

We're having so much fun, does he really need to take a nap?"

"Yes." mommy said, "Your brother is still a baby and he needs to take naps to grow big and strong."

As mommy was putting Geronimo to bed, Geraldine sat quietly on the couch looking sadly towards the window thinking, "I don't like rainy days. Rainy days are boring. What can I do?"

Suddenly, Geraldine had a **wonderful** idea.

"Mommy, can my friends Charlotte and Annabel come over to play?"

"Hmm ..." mommy said.

"Please, mommy!"

"All right." she replied. "I'll call and see if your friends can visit."

"Thank you, mommy!" Geraldine said cheerfully.

When Geraldine's friends arrived they went right to her room to play. Geraldine was so happy to be with her friends; they always had hours of fun when they were together. They played dress up, read stories to each other, and especially enjoyed playing with Geraldine's dollhouse.

After some time, Geraldine started to smell something delicious.

"I think I smell cookies!"

Geraldine said.

"So do I," said Charlotte.

"Me too," said Annabel.

"I'm hungry, let's get a snack," said Geraldine.

6

Off they went happily skipping to the kitchen. "Mommy, did you bake cookies?" asked Geraldine.

"Yes, I did. I just finished baking a batch of oatmeal chocolate chip cookies," mommy replied.

"My favourite!" said Geraldine.

"Yummy" said Charlotte.

"Thank you" said Annabel.

Geraldine and her friends sat around the table as mommy gave each a freshly baked cookie with a glass of milk. Baby Geronimo was seated in his highchair already munching on pieces of cookies that mommy had given him.

Before the girls started eating, Geraldine prayed, "Lord, thank you for this wonderful snack that mommy has prepared for us. Please provide for those who do not have anything to eat. In Jesus' name, Amen." Geraldine and her friends immediately started eating their snack. They enjoyed the cookies so much, they asked for more!

"What can we do now?" Annabel asked

"I know, let's go out in the rain!"

Geraldine said.

"Yay!" Charlotte and Annabel shouted.

"Mommy can we go play in the rain?" Geraldine asked.

"Well, it's not raining too hard, let's all go out for a walk." Mommy said. While mommy was dressing Geronimo, the girls eagerly put on their raincoats, rain boots and grabbed their umbrellas.

Off they went out in the rain. The girls were holding hands, galloping along, hopping over and into the puddles. They enjoyed the rain on their faces. They were giggling and laughing and having such a wonderful time. Geronimo was having a great time too as he watched the girls in amazement.

10

Finally, the rain stopped. The girls were a little disappointed as they were having lots of fun. Suddenly, Geraldine cried out,

"Look, over there, in the sky! It's a rainbow!"

They all looked up at the sky in total disbelief, how wonderful it was to look at a colourful rainbow.

"Wow!" the girls shouted.

"It's so beautiful!" Geraldine said with amazement. Their eyes were fixed on the rainbow until it slowly faded away.

"Come girls, let's head back home." Mommy said. They headed back home quietly, still surprised at what they had just seen.

Once they arrived home Geraldine had a wonderful idea. She dashed off to her room to get her art basket and dashed back to the kitchen. The basket was complete with crayons, colourful paints and paintbrushes.

"Let's paint a rainbow!"

Geraldine said excitedly.

"Yes!"

her friends answered.

Geraldine and her friends immediately started on their drawings. Mommy gave baby Geronimo paper and crayons to keep busy. Geraldine loved painting rainbows, she knew exactly which colors to use. Charlotte was already down to her last color and Annabel was gently stroking her paintbrush against the paper.

While mommy was baking a second batch of cookies, she asked;

"Who created rainbows?"

"God," the girls replied together.

"Does anybody remember which story in the Bible speaks about rainbows?" mommy asked.

"The story of Noah,"

Geraldine shouted.

"Yes," mommy said. "God promised Noah that He would never flood the earth again and that a rainbow would follow rain as a reminder that God keeps His promises."

"Aren't you glad God keeps His promises?"

"I know I am!"

"I am very grateful that I was able to see a lovely rainbow today."

"You know, I think I like rainy days after all!"

"I hope your rainy days will be as exciting as mine."

18

Dear Reader,

I have written a Bible verse for you to read and I have drawn a picture of a rainbow for you to color on your own!"

For a fun craft idea, draw a colourful rainbow on paper along with your name and age and send it to me at;

me@geraldinethegiraffe.org

Once I receive your drawing, I will post it on my website! You can visit me anytime at;

www.geraldinethegiraffe.org

Your friend,
Geraldine

ACKNOWLEDGEMENTS

I thank and praise the Lord for being the source of inspiration for this book.

"Your word is a lamp to my feet and a light for my path." (Psalm 119:105 NIV)

I want to thank family and friends for their thoughts and prayers.

A heartfelt thanks to Joanne, Lorraine and Fadi for their unfailing prayers and generous support.

CPSIA information can be obtained
at www.ICGtesting.com
Printed in the USA
245143LV00002BA